917.2
HOP

WITHDRAWN

SE POLK DELAWARE
ELEMENTARY LIBRARY

WORLD IN VIEW

MEXICO

Amanda Hopkinson

RAINTREE
STECK-VAUGHN
LIBRARY
The Steck-Vaughn Company

Austin, Texas

© Copyright 1992, text, Steck-Vaughn Company

All rights reserved. No reproduction, copy or transmission of this publication may be made without written permission from the publisher.

Library of Congress Cataloging-in-Publication Data

Hopkinson, Amanda, 1948–
   Mexico / Amanda Hopkinson.
      p.   cm.—(World in view)
   Includes index.
   Summary: Surveys the climate, wildlife, history, industry, culture, and other aspects of Mexico.
   ISBN 0-8114-2452-9
   1. Mexico—Juvenile literature. [1. Mexico.] I. Title.
   II. Series.
F1208.H68   1992   92-7815
972—dc20   CIP AC

Cover: *Pyramid of the Magician, Uxmal, Yucatán*
Title page: *Baja California landscape*

Design by Julian Holland Publishing Ltd.

Consultant: Bruce Taylor, University of Dayton

Typeset by Multifacit Graphics, Keyport, NJ
Printed and bound in the United States
by Lake Book, Melrose Park, IL
2 3 4 5 6 7 8 9 0 LB 96 95 94

Photographic credits
Cover: D. Donne Bryant; title page: Sean Sprague/Mexicolore, 7 Bruce Coleman Ltd, 8 Rubén Pax, 9, 12 Tony Morrison/South American Pictures, 14 Robert Harding Picture Library, 16 Rubén Pax, 17 Norman Owen Tomalin/Bruce Coleman Ltd, 18 Graciela Iturbide, 20, 22, 25, 27 Rubén Pax, 29 Tony Morrison/South American Pictures, 30 Rubén Pax, 34 Tony Morrison/South American Pictures, 36 Sean Sprague/Mexicolore, 38 Brian Moser/Hutchison Library, 40 Rubén Pax, 45 Tony Morrison/South American Pictures, 48 Popperfoto, 49 Tony Morrison/South American Pictures, 51 Popperfoto, 52 Sean Sprague/Mexicolore, 56 Kimball Morrison/South American Pictures, 58 Sean Sprague/Mexicolore, 61, 63 Tony Morrison/ South American Pictures, 65 Mexicolore, 66 Sean Sprague/Mexicolore, 67 Tony Morrison/ South American Pictures, 70 John Goldblatt/Mexicolore, 72 Tony Morrison/South American Pictures, 73 Sean Sprague/Mexicolore, 74 Liba Taylor/Hutchison Library, 78 Robert Harding Picture Library, 80, 83 Rubén Pax, 85 Tony Morrison/South American Pictures, 88 Sean Sprague/Mexicolore, 89 Rubén Pax, 92 Tony Morrison/South American Pictures, 94 Sean Sprague/South American Pictures.

Contents

1. Introducing Mexico 5
2. Plentiful and Varied Wildlife 17
3. Who Is a Mexican? 24
4. From Mythology to History 30
5. Spanish Rule and Mexican Independence 37
6. The Revolution and After 48
7. Industry and Agriculture 57
8. Travel in a Land of Mountains and Lakes 64
9. Health, Education, and Welfare 68
10. Home and Away 77
11. Religion and Culture 85
12. Mexico Today—and Tomorrow 90
    Index 95

MEXICO

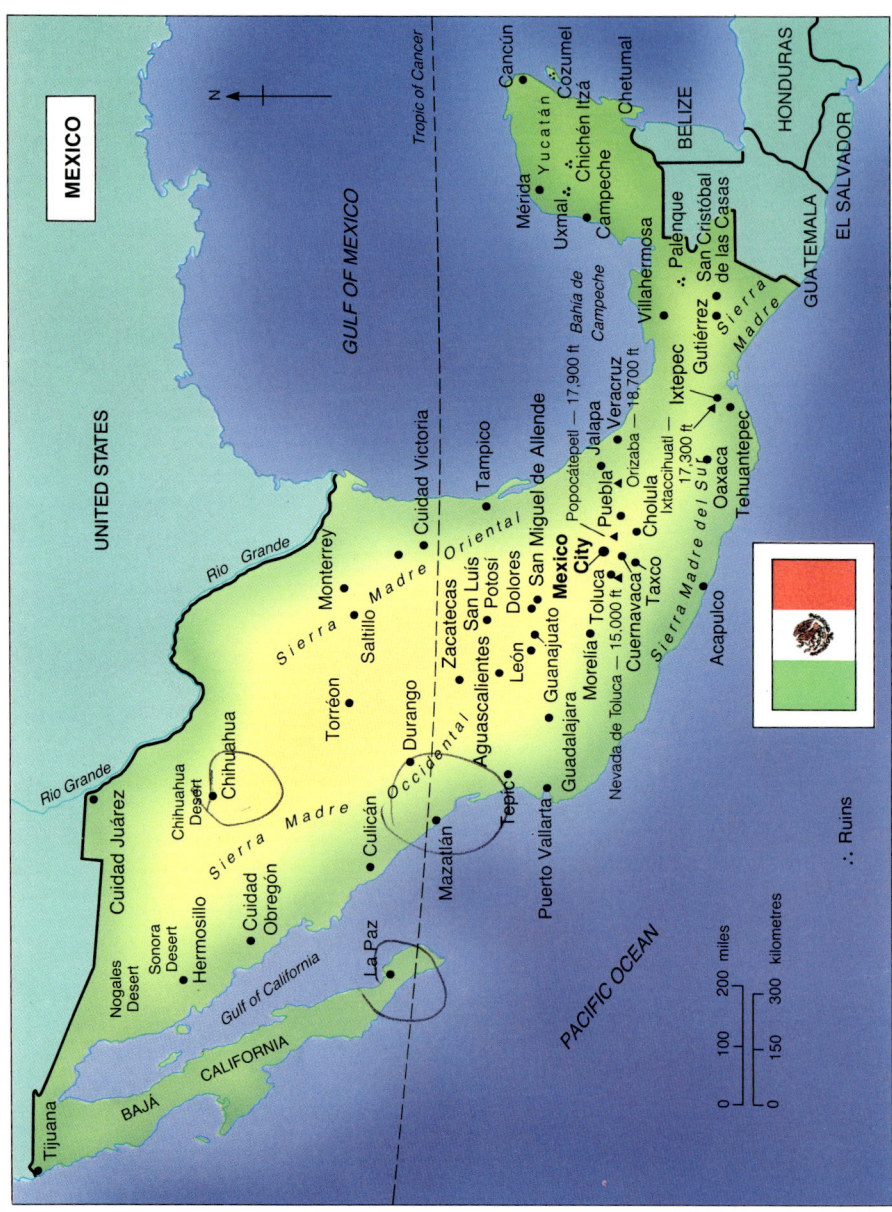

1 Introducing Mexico

Mexico is the northernmost country in the narrow neck of land linking North and South America. On a map Mexico appears to be in North America, but its people, language, and way of life are very similar to the countries in Central America. The frontiers of Mexico have changed frequently over many years, and there is a lot of discussion about where Mexico fits in the geography and culture of the Americas.

The Americas are made up of Canada, the United States, Central America, and South America. The people of Central and South America are often called "Latin Americans." This name is given to people from some areas in the Americas where Spanish, Portuguese, or French is spoken as the main language. In general, Latin Americans do not like the United States being called "America" because they say that the United States only covers part of North America, and Latin Americans feel that they have very

Mexico's Flag
Mexico's green, white, and red flag was designed by the nationalist movement in the nineteenth century. It is a symbol of independence, which was won in 1821. In the center is an eagle perched on a cactus, holding a squirming snake in its beak. According to Aztec Indian legend, the place where the eagle landed was where they should build Mexico's first capital, the city of Tenochtitlán, which is now called Mexico City.

MEXICO

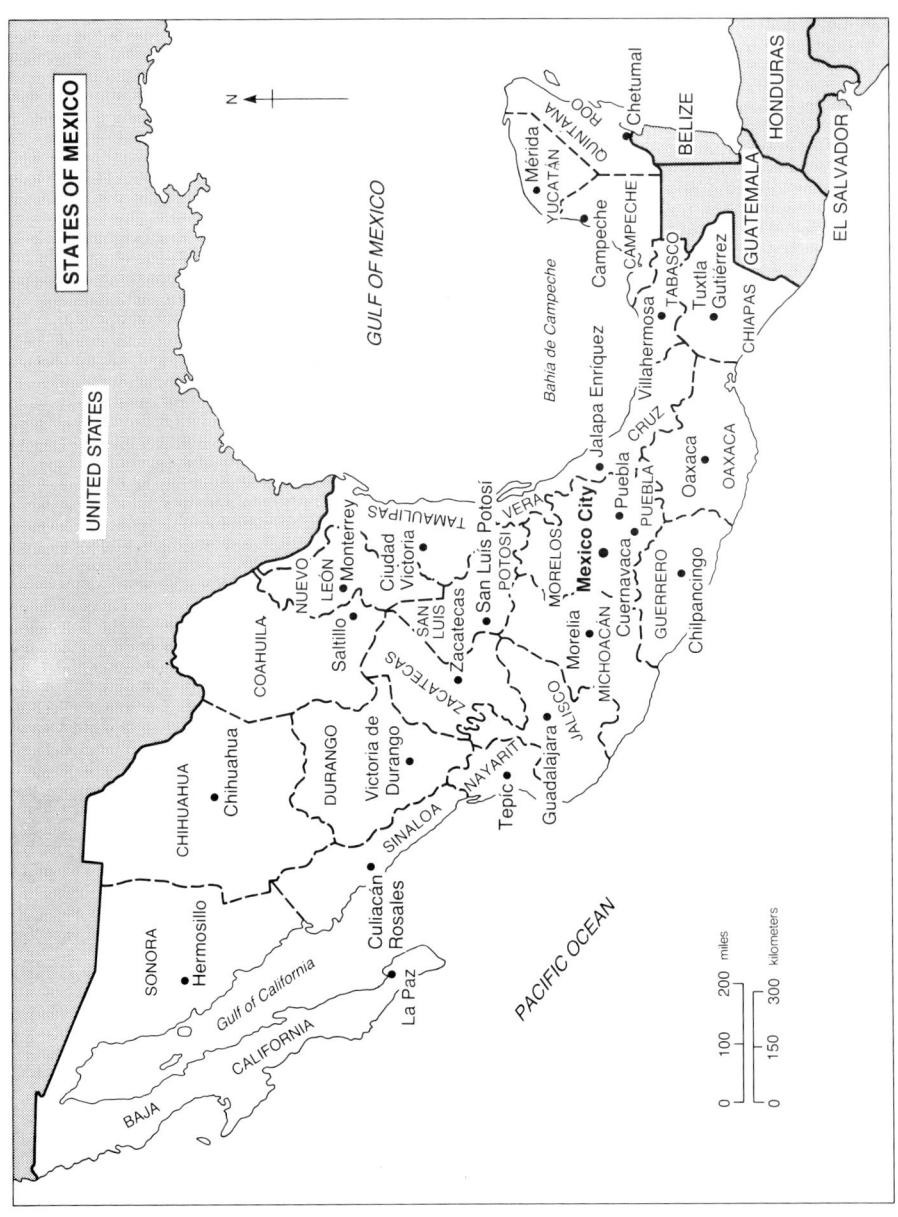

INTRODUCING MEXICO

separate cultures from those in the U.S. and Canada. The main language spoken in Mexico is Spanish, and Mexico therefore comes under the title of "Latin America."

New Spain
The Spanish invaded and conquered Mexico during the sixteenth and seventeenth centuries, introducing and spreading their language to the area as they took more and more control of the region. The Spanish also conquered land as far west as California, as far east as Florida, and as far north as Wyoming, including all of Texas and Arizona. As a result their language spread a long way into North America. With the people in all these areas speaking Spanish, it is not surprising that there has been confusion about where

The peninsula of Baja California stretches for over 621 miles (1,000 kilometers) down the Pacific coast of Mexico although it is only 62 miles (100 kilometers) wide for most of its length. It is a region of desert and arid mountains.

7

MEXICO

Mexico belongs in the Americas, and the names of some of the states in the U.S. and Mexico make the problem worse. One of the states in Mexico is called Baja California, which means Lower California, and one of the states in the United States is called New Mexico.

Natural boundaries
Natural boundaries now determine three of Mexico's borders. The Rio Grande River forms much of the northern border; the Gulf of Mexico and the Caribbean Sea act as the eastern border; and the Pacific Ocean serves as the western border. The northern border with the United States is 1,500 miles (2,400 kilometers) long. It is one of the longest borders between two countries anywhere in the world.

The Yucatán Peninsula on the eastern coast of Mexico has a climate similar to the islands of the Caribbean Sea. The rocky coast is fringed with palm trees and lush vegetation.

INTRODUCING MEXICO

The central square, or Zócalo, in Mexico City is a busy place. Over 600 people arrive in the city every day looking for work and a place to live.

Mexico's southern neighbors are Guatemala and Belize. Guatemala has an ancient Mayan culture that crosses the border into Mexico. Belize was ruled by the British until 1986, and English is the official language. Although Mexico has the most Spanish-speakers of anywhere in the world, there are powerful influences from English-speaking neighbors and from Mexicans who speak Native American languages.

Population

Mexico is the eleventh largest country in the world. Its overall population is thought to be about 88 million people. In 1965, the total population of the country was only 45 million. Mexico is the third largest country in Latin America after Brazil and Argentina, covering an area about a quarter the size of the U.S. Around

9

half the national population is under the age of 21, which makes Mexico one of the youngest and fastest-growing major nations in the world.

According to a census taken in 1989, the population of Mexico City has risen to approximately 20 million, which is the same as the entire population of this area when it was conquered in the sixteenth century by Spain. The last estimate before that was taken in 1987, and put the total number of people in Mexico City at 18.1 million. The national birth rate is now a major problem, with the population growing by 1.5 million (2.4 percent) each year.

Natural features
The Caribbean coastline around the Gulf of Mexico is 1,700 miles (2,790 kilometers) long, and the Pacific coast around the Gulf of California extends over 4,600 miles (7,360 kilometers). Two mountain ranges, called the Sierra Madre Oriental and the Sierra Madre Occidental, stretch along the eastern and western seaboards. These act as natural boundaries to a great central plateau. Hernán Cortés, the leader of the Spanish army that conquered Mexico, crumpled a piece of parchment into a mass of peaks and crevices to illustrate his description of Mexico. The mountains are also natural barriers to communications, and most of the roads and railroads have to run north-south along the floor of the plains. In the north of Mexico there are the vast deserts of Nogales, Sonora, and Chihuahua and in the south of the country are the lush tropical and forested regions of Oaxaca and Chiapas. However, in the Chiapas region, in

INTRODUCING MEXICO

> **The coast**
> The east coast of Mexico is the home of most of the ports in the country. It is also the richest agricultural and cattle-raising region of the country, and an area noted for its sulfur and oil mining. On the Pacific coast, the seaports are mainly known as tourist resorts and the infertile land, where crops do not usually grow, has only recently been used to grow grapes for the production of wines.

particular, the forests are rapidly being cut down and soil erosion and ecological destruction are becoming serious problems.

There is a rich variety of land in Mexico. It ranges from swamp to desert, from arid highlands that are very dry and have only alpine vegetation growing on them to areas so lush that three crops can be grown annually. Over half the country is higher than 3,280 feet (1,000 meters), most of it over 6,560 feet (2,000 meters). Half is classified as arid and nearly another third as semiarid. Only 16 percent of every 74 million acres (30 million hectares) of land can be used to grow crops, and only a third of this area is suitable for water to be supplied to it by artificial means, such as canals or waterways.

Volcanoes and earthquakes

Volcanoes are another typical feature of the land in Mexico, and of Central America as a whole. The land in the middle of the country is ringed with alternating lakes and basins encircled with volcanoes. The highest volcanoes are Orizaba,

MEXICO

There are many volcanoes in Mexico. In the Sierra Madre Occidental is the Nevado de Toluca, one of the highest volcanoes in all of Mexico.

which is 18,700 feet (5,700 meters) high; Popocatépetl, which is 17,900 feet (5,452 meters) high; Ixtaccihuatl, which is 17,300 feet (5,286 meters) high; and the Nevado de Toluca, which is 15,000 feet (4,583 meters) high. All of these are now either dormant and have not erupted for many years (although they might one day), or they are extinct, which means that they will never erupt again. These volcanoes form the basins of such major cities as Guadalajara and Toluca as well as the capital, Mexico City.

The area of volcanoes is called the "heart of Mexico." It covers only 14 percent of the country but has ample rainfall and is home to nearly half the entire population. The Mexico City basin with its 20 million inhabitants only covers an area of 31

INTRODUCING MEXICO

square miles (50 square kilometers). Mexico City also lies on the San Andreas faultline, which is famous for some of the most devastating earthquakes in the world this century. Earthquakes are vibrations caused when rocks deep in the Earth move. Sometimes pressure builds up under the Earth's surface on a faultline, where two rock masses meet, and the rocks jerk forward, causing an earthquake. The San Andreas faultline runs from the San Francisco Bay area down through central Mexico. Two major earthquakes have shocked Mexico City in the space of a generation: one in 1956 and one in 1985. There have also been many minor ones.

The other natural disasters to which Mexico is subject are typhoons and hurricanes, which sweep west through the Gulf of Mexico. Typhoons and hurricanes are violent storms with very strong winds. The offshore islands of Mexico and the Yucatán Peninsula are areas particularly affected by these storms.

The climate

Generally speaking, the days are hot and nights relatively cool in Mexico. There are, however, three separate types of temperature zones. There is a zone called the "hotlands," or *tierra caliente*, which includes the coastlands and the area of central plateau below 2,460 feet (750 meters); temperate zones, or the *tierra templada*, cover land from 2,460 to 6,562 feet (750 to 2,000 meters) high; and a cold zone, the *tierra fría*, runs from 6,562 feet (2,000 meters) and up.

Mexico is known as a country of "climatic pockets." Each pocket is an area that has its own

MEXICO

The land and air in the desert region of Coahuila is dry. It supports a little scrub and poor grass on which a few cattle can graze. Any storms that come usually bring no rain, only dust and sand.

levels of humidity and moisture, and of heat and rainfall, and also its own type and texture of soil. In most areas May to July are the hottest months, with both Mexico City and Villahermosa having temperatures of up to 76° to 85°F (27° to 30°C). In the winter, the difference between the two cities widens, with the temperature in Mexico City dropping to 69°F (19°C) and the temperature in Villahermosa dropping to about 75°F (26°C).

Temperature is affected by latitude, which is the position of a place north or south of the equator. The Tropic of Cancer, which marks the northern edge of areas with a constantly hot tropical climate, runs across the center of Mexico, so the overall temperature is very warm. However, temperature is also affected by altitude, which is the height above sea level, and Mexico

City, at a height of 7,800 feet (2,380 meters), has a mild and pleasant climate.

The amount of rainfall varies widely. In the northwest only 2 inches (50 mm) of rain may fall in an entire year, while in the southeast the same amount may fall in one day of tropical storms. Baja California and the Sonora desert have less than 10 inches (250 mm) of annual rainfall, while most of northern Mexico down to the capital has almost twice as much in a year.

The seasons

Summer is from June to August and winter is from November to January. The summer is the wet season and the winter is the dry season, and there are only two areas where the rain falls all year round. One is the area along the Pacific coast of the southern state of Chiapas, and the other is the area from the lower slopes of the Sierra Madre Oriental across the narrow neck of land from Tehuantepec to Villahermosa.

The regional variations in temperature and rainfall mean that the amount of vegetation differs from area to area. It is too cold for trees to grow over 13,124 feet (4,000 meters) high, for instance. Above the treeline there are only extremely bare highland heaths. In most of northern Mexico there is little agriculture and hardly enough pasture for animals. Skeletons of cattle and horses attest to the rigors of life in the region. Windmills are still used to provide what water there is, and new irrigation systems are being built to help peasant farmers.

The climates of Veracruz in the east and Acapulco in the west have a lot of similarities and

MEXICO

The Río Usumacinta is a large river flowing through the dense forests of the Chiapas region. These tropical forests support a huge range of wildlife, but their habitat is threatened because many trees have been felled in recent years.

therefore the vegetation in each place is similar. Both areas are tropical, being moist, hot, and crowded with vegetation. Banana palms grow particularly well in Veracruz and Acapulco. If you travel overland between these two cities you can leave behind the sea-level tropics in the morning; pass through a cold, and sometimes freezing, temperature at high noon; and reach the humid tropics again on the other side of the range by the same night. The land and vegetation, the crops and animals, vary enormously, from zones of permanent snow to ones of continuous warmth.

Plentiful and Varied Wildlife

Mexican animals are masters of disguise. The chameleon and its close relatives, lizards and iguanas, are native inhabitants and are either capable of changing color according to their background or are dappled so as to blend in with the background and are difficult to see. Also, the only two kinds of poisonous lizard in the world are both found in Mexico. One is the "beaded lizard," which is patterned in a way resembling strung beads and can grow up to three feet long in its native habitat of western Mexico. The other, the "Gila monster," is a near relative and neighbor

The "keel-billed" toucan is one of over 30 varieties found in Central and South America. These noisy birds are found in the tropical forests of Mexico and neighboring countries.

MEXICO

This woman is carrying iguanas to market. These harmless lizards are a popular food in Mexico.

of the beaded lizard, with similarly beaded-looking scales. Both the lizards have a poisonous bite that can hurt and make people ill, though neither could kill a person. Iguanas are completely harmless to people, but people can be extremely harmful to them. Throughout Mexico, the iguana is hunted, roasted, and eaten as a delicacy and a rich source of protein.

Birds and butterflies

Migrating birds and butterflies are commonplace, many flying down from as far as Canada. Some species spend the winter in the woods of central Mexico. Sometimes, many hundreds cluster together in one tree. Some of the butterflies are

PLENTIFUL AND VARIED WILDLIFE

larger than birds, particularly the tiny hummingbirds whose whirring wings can make them seem blurred and difficult to see. The best time to see hummingbirds is when they pause on some exotic flower to draw the nectar through their surprisingly long beaks.

While there are often problems in telling some of the birds from some of the vegetation, others vary brilliantly with their surroundings. These tend to be the birds that can fly from human sight into thick tropical jungle. They include scarlet and yellow parakeets, parrots, macaws, and black-and-white toucans with their huge vividly striped bills. The bill of a toucan is like that of a pelican and is big enough to carry food to its young. The toucans' bills are so dangerously curved that if two become locked together during fights over territory or during the mating season, they can have a lot of trouble breaking free!

Over the northern deserts the most common species of bird are birds of prey. There are many types of eagles, including the rare and beautiful golden eagle that nests in narrow openings and cracks in rocks. Hawks and buzzards scan the sands of the deserts for smaller birds and rodents to eat, and ugly bald-headed vultures venture as far as city dumps, where they scavenge for food alongside the poor people of the area who need to do so. In all, Mexico is home to at least 1,400 different bird species.

Animal life on the land

Some animals make their presence known by their sounds. There are many kinds of chattering monkeys, including the black howler, which is

19

MEXICO

This is a howler monkey. They live in large groups in the forests of Mexico and Central America. Howler monkeys are thought to be the noisiest animals in the world. Their howl can be heard for many miles.

perhaps the noisiest in the world and also performs tricks swinging upside-down by its tail. Other upside-down creatures in Mexico include furry fruit-tree sloths, which earned their name because they sleep during the day, and that other strange night prowler, the bat. Vampire bats live in the tropical jungles and get their name from their bloodsucking habits. They like their prey to be hairless and will attack sleeping humans when possible. The front incisors of vampire bats let out a type of mild anesthetic that numbs the flesh so that their prey doesn't wake up when the skin is pierced and blood drained. Although it is almost impossible to bleed to death from such small bites or incisions, early travelers' tales are full of details about prey being weakened by attacks from bats a few nights in a row.

PLENTIFUL AND VARIED WILDLIFE

Animal life in the sea and rivers

In all, Mexico boasts over 500 different kinds of native mammals. These include the gray whale, which is born in sheltered bays of the Pacific Ocean off Baja California. Each baby weighs half a ton and drinks as much as 52 gallons (200 liters) of its mother's milk daily. Fifty years ago, many whales were being killed, giving rise to fears that this particular mammal would soon be extinct, but the hunting of certain kinds of whales is now illegal and the whales are further protected by strict rules.

Overfishing has also affected the amount of fish on both coastlines of Mexico, and river pollution is now a real and growing problem. Fishermen in Mexico export a lot of shellfish to foreign countries. Lobsters, crayfish, and giant Pacific prawns are the shellfish most in demand for export. Oysters are also very popular in foreign countries, where they are a luxury. They are not a luxury in Mexico itself, however. Oysters are part of the ordinary Mexican's diet. Exotic, sparkling like jewels, and often luminous, tiny fish dart about the coral reefs, sponge plants, and delicately colored sea anemones. Mexico is also host to over 260 species of amphibians, which live in and out of the water, and 680 kinds of reptiles, including alligators.

Plants and crops

As with animals, so with plants: there is a wealth not only of different varieties but also of differences to be found within each variety. There are more orchids and cacti in Mexico than in any other single country, and the same may be true of

MEXICO

The cactus plant is common throughout Mexico and, in spite of its prickly exterior, has many uses. There is an enormous variety of cacti. This one is providing shade for a roadside vendor.

bananas and chili peppers. It is said that there are 50 varieties of cacti and 100 kinds of chili peppers in Mexico. The sap of some cacti is used to brew alcohol. The fruit and stems of prickly pear cactus are cooked and eaten. The stems of certain cacti contain a sisallike thread that can be woven into hammocks, mats, and even clothes.

Corn and beans form the staple diet of even the poorest Mexicans, with perhaps *tunas*, which is the fruit of the prickly pear cactus, for dessert. In rural families, other fruits and vegetables may be gathered or harvested to take to market. These crops include wild custard apples, persimmons, or *zapote*, which is a strange, squashy black fruit with giant-sized seeds. More familiar fruits and vegetables include carefully cultivated tomatoes, melons, and oranges. Mexico has such a range of tropical and temperate areas that while in some regions guava, mango, and papaya are commonplace, in others there are apple orchards and strawberry fields.

Fruits are often sold by peasants on street corners or marketplaces, stacked in little piles, for a price that excludes the customary politeness of an additional *pilón*, or tip, as the goods are handed over. Flowers also make good merchandise. Flower markets are full of large, flat baskets with bunches of long-stemmed gladioli or lilies and garlands of bougainvillea and jasmine. Although picking rare varieties of orchid is strictly forbidden, some commercial varieties are grown in lakes, on rafts laid just under the surface for bulbs and seedlings. Water lilies and decorative rushes are sold at the waterside. In the southwestern state of Oaxaca, where there are many lakes, flower markets are still held on rafts lashed together with reeds, just as they once were in the Aztec capital in the central basin.

3 Who Is a Mexican?

Opinions differ over whether the first inhabitants of the narrow neck of land linking North and South America trekked south from the icy Alaskan wastes or sailed from the sunny Polynesian islands. Woolly mammoth remains, such as those found in the central basin of Mexico not long ago, hint at the former, while features of ancient sculptures, made by the Olmec people who lived from 1200 B.C. to A.D. 250, seem to resemble those on Easter Island in the Pacific. Some people even assumed that Mexican pyramids meant that early residents must have arrived from Egypt! This theory is now largely discounted since, on taking a closer look at the pyramids, it was decided that they were differently constructed and built thousands of years later.

The Indians

Whether these people arrived by trekking overland from the north or sailing over the western ocean, they became the native people of Mexico. It was Columbus, when he arrived in the Bahama Islands in 1492, who first called the native people of America "Indians." Columbus believed that he had sailed a good part of the way around the world from his home port in Spain. He assumed that he had finally reached his destination—the "Indies," which he believed to be located near Japan. So naturally, if erroneously, he referred to the gentle people he found there as Indians.

WHO IS A MEXICAN?

This family in the market in Puebla have the typical flat features, broad lips, and wide noses of the Puebla Indians.

the Zapoteca of Oaxaca, are matriarchal, which means that women control the economy and society. In these societies men are expected to be more caring and do as the women ask them.

The Spaniards

Although the Spaniards ruled the Indians after 1519 and often used them as slaves, their numbers were very small compared to the native populations. They gained power through a combination of their superior weapons and the refusal of certain Indian peoples to become warlike and engage in battle. After they had gained control, the Spanish began to settle. Over the following centuries, thousands of people from Spain made the perilous voyage to Mexico. Nearly all of these people were men, and in time, they and their fellow European adventurers intermarried with Indian women. The people who came from Spain dominated the rest, and they imposed Spanish as the national language. It was estimated in 1990 that about 90 percent of the Mexican population were of mixed race, and now 97 percent of these people speak at least some Spanish, even where other indigenous languages are also preserved.

A mixed race

A mixed race, *mestizo*, is the cornerstone of present-day Mexican identity. Originally it signified the mixture of Indian with Hispanic (a person of Spanish descent). Many portraits and pages of writing were devoted by seventeenth- and eighteenth-century settlers to describing different variations of racial mixtures in Mexico. Where there were relatively few Indians, slaves were imported from Africa via the West Indian islands to work for the Hispanic people. They worked as personal servants, as mine workers, and as overseers for Indian workers. In time, black slaves and Hispanics intermarried. A child born to a black and a Hispanic was called *mulatto*.

Despite intermarriage, for many years Indians and blacks were generally looked down upon as inferiors by Hispanics, particularly by those born in Spain rather than in Mexico. Although slavery

WHO IS A MEXICAN?

There are many people of mixed race in Mexico and each variation has a name. The man pumping gas is a mulatto, *which means that one of his parents was black and the other of Spanish origin.*

was formally abolished after Mexican independence in 1829, blacks and Indians lived in servitude as *péons*, or serfs.

The 1910 Revolution

Effective change only came with the 1910 Revolution. The two greatest leaders of the revolution were of Indian blood. The system of government and laws, known as a constitution, set up by the revolution guaranteed the human and civic rights of every member of the population. Mexicans remain enormously proud of the spirit of justice that inspired their revolution. This spirit of nationalism, the mingling of races, and a common language are all major parts of every Mexican's identity.

MEXICO

4 From Mythology to History

History tends to be thought of as what has been written down and mythology to be what has been passed on by word of mouth. Both are concerned with the same subject matter: the origins of people, in particular their family and social organization at different periods in time, and accounts of their travels and trials.

The Aztec and the Maya
The Aztecs were the Indian people dominant in central Mexico at the time of the Spanish invasion. Before them, numerous civilizations had risen and fallen, often with no clear record of precisely when and why. It has been possible to

Palenque is the site of a Mayan city, part of which has this splendid temple. The priests of the temples were also the rulers, so Mayan temples were beautifully built and handsomely decorated.

30

FROM MYTHOLOGY TO HISTORY

discern both from tales and myths and from remaining records of the period, such as those found on stone slabs in various regions of the country, that the Olmec people were dominant from 1200 B.C. to about A.D. 250. At this point the Zapotecs and Maya became the dominant peoples for nearly 700 years. These were followed by the Toltec civilization, which lasted from A.D. 900 to 1200.

By far the most important of these peoples were the Maya. The descendants of the Maya still live in the Mexican Yucatán and Chiapas and far down into Guatemala. However, they are now divided into many distinct language groups. The Maya created the impressive and extensive cities of Uxmal, Chichén Itzá, and Palenque to house governmental and religious institutions. Religion permeated every aspect of Mayan life, including rites and ceremonies, art forms, and even team games the exact significance of which still remains a mystery.

The Maya developed a high degree of mathematical and scientific skills and an extensive knowledge of astronomy. They also developed a complex form of writing using symbols called "hieroglyphs." For many years Maya writings remained largely secret and untranslatable. But recently scholars have made great advances in deciphering the Maya writing system. The fascinating story of the great Maya civilization is now emerging from mythology into a true written history.

It is not known why the Maya's great cities seem to have been suddenly abandoned in the tenth century and were never again inhabited.

Was it a plague or some other natural disaster that drove the people away? Or was it a dire religious warning that made it unthinkable for such a people who believed in fate to remain? Experts today, with their new ability to decipher Maya writings, are exploring the possibility that terribly destructive warfare was the reason for the collapse of Maya civilization.

The Aztecs emerged as the dominant nation in the central Mexican plateau during the fourteenth century. They were a warlike people who had a theocratic religion that demanded daily human sacrifice. The Aztecs developed a high degree of civilization, and by the time the Spanish arrived they ruled an area with a population estimated to be about 20 million.

The arrival of the Spanish

When the Spaniards came to Central America, they burned a wealth of native manuscripts, destroying recorded mythical histories. However, it is known that the Aztecs believed in a great winged serpent as their redeemer, which they called Quetzalcóatl. Like Christians who believe in Jesus's Second Coming, the Aztecs thought Quetzalcóatl would return one day across the seas from the east, escorted by a pale-skinned figure with a bearded face. When the Spanish *conquistador*, or conqueror, Hernán Cortés, arrived with 500 men at Veracruz on the eastern coast in 1519 and journeyed into the interior of the country, messengers went ahead of them to tell the Aztec ruler, Moctezuma, of their arrival. The Spanish messengers, who at first were assumed by the Aztecs to be joined to their

FROM MYTHOLOGY TO HISTORY

> **Spanish Colonization**
> In the late fifteenth century, several things resulted in the Spanish colonization of the Americas. One was the development of sturdy oceangoing ships that could be used by explorers and adventurers, such as Magellan, Marco Polo, and Vasco da Gama, to seek the vast continents of India and Cathay, which we now call China. They believed that these continents could be reached by sailing west from Europe. Spain also developed plans not only for colonization but for Christianization. The Catholic monarchs, King Ferdinand and Queen Isabella, who wished to make Spain Christian again, had waged a civil war against the Moorish forces still holding power over sections of the Spanish peninsula. They planned to give the Moors, followers of Islam, and the Jews the option of death or conversion. Christopher Columbus, an Italian adventurer, approached the Spanish court in 1490, at just the right moment to win support for his projects of exploration. The Catholic monarchs approved an extension of their imperial and Christianizing mission overseas, with the blessing of Pope Alexander VI, also a Spaniard.

horses, creatures new to the natives, were welcomed as fulfilment of Aztec prophecy.

The Aztecs ruled over many tribes, and there was a good deal of dissension between the Aztecs and these tribes. Cortés saw in this unrest an opportunity to destroy the empire. In November 1519 he and his army arrived in the Aztec capital city, Tenochtitlán. The superstitious Moctezuma received the Spanish as descendants of the god

MEXICO

The Spanish soldier Hernán Cortés arrived to conquer Mexico in 1519. The guns and horses of the Spanish army, neither of which the Indians had seen before, gave Cortés's troops a great advantage and in a few years they had subdued most of the country.

Quetzalcóatl. Cortés took advantage of this and, taking Moctezuma hostage, he occupied Tenochtitlán and attempted to govern the Aztecs through him.

In the spring of 1520, when Cortés was away commanding an expedition, a rough and mistrustful Spanish soldier, Pedro de Alvarado, slaughtered hundreds of Aztecs in fear of a possible uprising. Soon after Cortés's return, the Aztec people did indeed rise and surround the Spanish. Many of the Spanish were killed as they

> **Cortés's Impression of Tenochtitlán, the Aztec Capital of Mexico**
> "This great city was built on a salt lake, and no matter by what road you travel there are two leagues from the main body of the city to the mainland. There are four artificial causeways leading to it, and each is as wide as two cavalry lances . . . there are bridges made of long and wide beams joined together very firmly and so well made that on some of them ten horsemen may ride abreast. . . .
>
> This city has many squares where trading is done. . . . There is also one square . . . with arcades all around, where more than 60,000 people come each day to buy and sell, and where every kind of merchandise produced in these lands is found; provisions as well as ornaments of gold and silver, lead, brass, copper, tin, stones, shells, bones, and feathers. . . . Each kind of merchandise is sold in its own street without any mixture whatever; they are very particular in this. Everything is sold by number and size, and until now I have seen nothing sold by weight. There is in this great square a very large building like a courthouse, where ten or twelve persons sit as judges. They preside over all that happens in the markets, and sentence criminals."

fought their way out of the capital city. This battle happened on June 30, 1520, and became known as the *noche triste*, which means "night of sorrow." The blood of the dying and wounded people was said to have stained the waters of the lake around Tenochtitlán red.

Six months later, Cortés returned with reinforcements, including units of Tlaxcalans,

MEXICO

Tenochtitlán was the Aztec capital. In this detail of a mural by Diego Rivera, the city is clearly shown. It was built on a group of islands in Lake Texcoco. At the time the Spanish arrived the capital was more magnificent and thirteen times larger than Paris, then the most important city in Europe.

long-standing enemies of the Aztecs. Together with other smaller groups of Indians, they soon surrounded and besieged the city that Cortés had at first found to be a model of beauty and civilization. The Spanish-led armies had two advantages over the Aztecs that they could not overcome: one was the speed and height the Spanish gained by riding horses, and the other was gunpowder. Though the heavy muskets and cannon of the Spanish look clumsy and primitive today, no amount of skill in sword fighting or firing arrows by the Aztecs could withstand them. In August 1521, Tenochtitlán, the great capital of the Aztecs, was finally surrendered to irresistible force.

5 Spanish Rule and Mexican Independence

During the sixteenth and seventeenth centuries the Spanish moved into more territories and settled throughout the Americas. Wars aimed at conquering the whole Indian race were waged against the indigenous peoples at several different times during the period. When the fighting at last came to an end, the Indians had become a subordinate people. Most of them worked for their conquerors, paid taxes to them, and adopted their religion.

Land ownership
The basic unit of wealth soon became the land. Holding land and distributing land and crops became the source of power for the Spanish, and led to repression of the workers. Soon the traditional system of several people holding land together and farming communally, which had been set up and practiced by the Indians, was given very little importance. The Spanish wanted individual people to own private property.

Land was divided by the Spaniards either into *ranchos*, which were privately owned farms, or into *haciendas,* which were owned by major landowners. The ranches and haciendas were run in a similar way to both the medieval manor in Europe and slave plantations in the southern U.S. In many regions, the two systems of

MEXICO

After the Spanish conquest large areas of land were divided up among the Spaniards. In fertile regions like Chiapas the large open spaces were turned into ranches where cattle were bred and a range of crops were grown.

landownership overlapped, but generally on ranches there were different types of crops grown and animals raised, whereas on haciendas only one thing was produced in great amounts. Some ranches had such a sufficient variety of goods that the people who lived on them could live on what they produced without buying from anywhere else. On haciendas, however, the owners either produced a single crop on a huge plantation; raised cattle, sheep, or horses on an extensive ranching area; or their major product came from mines on their property.

The amount and type of people needed to work on haciendas varied widely. For example, on cotton or coffee plantations farming work tended to be seasonal. Workers were needed mainly at

SPANISH RULE AND MEXICAN INDEPENDENCE

planting and harvest times, and wages were extremely low. Only a relatively few cowboys were needed to tend the animals even on vast areas of land. In the mines, however, a great many people were needed to work at all times.

> **Plantations**
>
> From the start Mexico's main plantations produced the "three Cs"—cane, cotton, and coffee. Later palm fruits, particularly bananas, were added. By the nineteenth century, competition over cotton was fiercest with the southern U.S. At times untreated cotton from the U.S. was two-thirds less expensive than Mexican cotton. Also U.S. interests, particularly in the form of the United Fruit Company, were controlling major export markets.
>
> Working conditions improved little overall in the centuries following the Spanish conquest. The great Church estates were expropriated by major landlords, who in turn found their lands seized to raise government funds for the wars of the late nineteenth and early twentieth centuries. None of these shifts in land ownership benefited the Indian population who, with a minority of Caribbean blacks, were forced to work the land.
>
> Typically, they would be forced off their own lands in the process of major land partitions, then they or other villagers would be imported back to work the plantations in conditions of virtual slavery. Since the work was seasonal, families would either have to travel and work together to earn a minimal wage, resulting in gross exploitation of child labor, or the male head of the family would leave behind wife and children for weeks or months on end to work far from home.

MEXICO

None of these systems proved beneficial for the Indians. The Spaniards made use of the native people only when it suited their own needs. Also, even when they weren't using the people for their own gain, they were using the land that had once belonged to the Indians.

Religion and culture

The earliest conquerors had arrived in Mexico with the slogan "The cross always follows the sword," and they began to introduce their religious beliefs to the Indians once they had gained control. Cortés went into battle led by a monk carrying a crucifix. In this way he showed his intention to conquer by winning hearts, minds, and souls as well as by taking over land.

The Spanish soldiers were also accompanied

Spanish missionaries coerced many of the native people into adopting Christianity. However, much of the Indians' own culture and some of their ideas were adapted into their Christianity. In Michoacán during Holy Week, the crucifixion is reenacted. The Roman soldiers are dressed like Spanish conquistadores.

SPANISH RULE AND MEXICAN INDEPENDENCE

by monks who baptized large numbers of Indians who did not really understand what was being done to them. These monks did not often go through the long process of teaching the Indians about their religion before converting them. They often held mass-baptisms for the Indians, who were persuaded to convert by the clever monks and the seeming invincibility of the Spanish conquest.

There were soon sharp differences of opinion between the views of the Spanish political leaders and the spiritual leaders on how Mexico's indigenous peoples should be treated. Some people in Spain asserted that Indians, like animals, had no souls, while the Catholic Church said that the Indians had "the souls of children." The Church often sought to protect the Indians. It made efforts to protect the traditional land rights of the Indians, but their actions were largely doomed to failure. This was partly because the missionary groups were often new Spanish arrivals and introduced yet more diseases to which the Indians were unaccustomed. These diseases attacked the Indians whom the missionaries wished to protect. In some cases, particularly under the Dominican and later the Jesuit fathers, this protection led to separate communities being set up for Indians who did not wish to become slaves or serfs.

The control the Spaniards held over land and Indians was closely linked to political power. The harsh way in which the Indians were treated led to constant and growing friction between the Spanish and the Indians during the 300 years of Spanish rule. On the other hand, Spain gave

Mexico a real and living part of its heritage. Although the social and political system was unfair, there were individuals who made a genuine contribution in cultural and spiritual ways in Mexico. The mixing of the different cultures has given Mexico some colonial towns with very fine architecture. Mexico also has a proud reputation in such varied art forms as poetry, music, dance, painting, pottery, and embroidery, which all developed into a distinctive style as the cultures of the two races merged.

It seems that much beauty developed in Mexico at a time when the indigenous people were suffering under the rule of their conquerors. When miners were experiencing poor working conditions and long hours, for example, the Church was using gold and silver for decorating the newly built churches. The Indians often paid with their lives to create things of permanent beauty. The Church gained the gold and silver for their churches from the mines in which the Indians worked and died. Again, it appears that, while the Church was trying to protect the Indians from the Spanish rulers, they were adding to the suffering of the Indians without realizing it, just as the missionaries had done when they brought disease to the country.

It is strange to consider what the Aztecs and Maya would have made of criticism of their "barbarism" by the Spanish, who stole their treasured manuscripts, instruments, and works of art by using force, in order to burn them; their jewelry and designs in silver and gold, in order to melt them down.

SPANISH RULE AND MEXICAN INDEPENDENCE

Spanish political ventures

Spain's political ventures were doomed in many ways. A curious law, written in 1571, sought to retain Mexican society in the form it was at that time and allow for no change. It dictated that only the Spanish aristocracy should govern Mexico. In other words, no Indian or black, no mestizo or mulatto, not even a Mexican-born Spaniard (a white *criollo*), could govern in his own country. The Spanish leaders acted as if there was a limitless supply of Spanish-born people in Mexico who were loyal to the Spanish crown.

This law placed even more strain on the social system in Mexico. It further separated the wealthy, Spanish-born landowning class, which held the political power, and the depressed laboring class. In particular, though, it increased the antagonism between the whites born in Spain (*gachupines*) and the criollos. With the growth of the mestizo population, it was only a matter of time before the opponents of the landowning class joined forces against them.

The struggle for independence

The national holiday that every Mexican schoolchild remembers is September 16, which is Independence Day. It was on this date in 1810 that a priest named Miguel Hidalgo y Costilla gathered an army of 80,000 people together under the slogan "Perish the Spaniards." There followed an eleven-year-long bloody civil war. Mexican independence was finally proclaimed by General Agustín de Iturbide in 1821. This independence swiftly became spoiled by personal ambition when General Iturbide

MEXICO

> **Father Miguel Hidalgo**
> His home town of Dolores Hidalgo is known as "the cradle of Mexican independence," and it is still considered proper for every new president to pay his respects there and repeat Father Miguel's proclamation of liberty. The *Grito de Dolores*, which literally means the "Shout of Dolores," was made in the early hours of September 16, 1810. It awoke a sleepy congregation to the birth of the independence movement. For Father Miguel, politics derived from morality, and he was always a priest first and politician after. Despite the fact that he had no military training, at one stage his peasant forces controlled nearly all of west-central Mexico. After being arrested by foreign troops, Father Hidalgo died by firing squad, and his head was displayed as a warning.

declared himself emperor the following year. Then, in 1824, a federal republic was declared by another general named Guadalupe Victoria, who was elected president. Similar power struggles between different leaders who wanted to control Mexico continued for the next thirty years.

Meanwhile, the northern Mexican provinces sought to separate into individual countries. In 1836, Texas declared its independence from Mexico, but nine years later it joined the U.S. War erupted between Mexico and the U.S. which led to the humiliating occupation of Mexico City by forces of the U.S. in 1847. In 1848 the Treaty of Guadalupe Hidalgo was signed. Under this treaty the U.S. received land that now comprises the states of Utah, Nevada, and California; most

SPANISH RULE AND MEXICAN INDEPENDENCE

of Arizona and New Mexico; and part of Wyoming and Colorado. The Rio Grande was declared to be the boundary between Mexico and Texas.

Benito Juárez and reform

Benito Juárez, a pure Zapotec Indian, became an important national hero in Mexico's long struggle

A statue to Benito Juárez, Mexico's first Indian president, was erected outside the headquarters of the ruling party in Mexico City. Juárez is nicknamed the ''Savior of Mexico.''

for independence and reform. His birthday, March 21, is celebrated by the entire country. He is nicknamed "the Savior of Mexico." It was Benito Juárez who, as president from 1857 to 1872, brought in a brief but important period of liberal reform. His reforms separated church and state, allowing for state-run education, civil marriage, and such rights as freedom of speech and of the press. This was popular with many people but it also outraged others, such as the conservatives, including many of Mexico's devout Catholics. The conservatives were inspired as much by their Christian beliefs as their political beliefs and did not like the idea of the church and state being separated. These feelings led to a civil war known as the "Three Years War."

European intervention
The European powers of Spain, France, and Britain watched the situation carefully. Although Juárez was victorious over his enemies, his government suffered financially. Foreign debts mounted when trade links with Europe were disrupted and the incoming revenues could not match the costs of the war. When Juárez halted payments on the foreign debt, joint Spanish, French, and British forces landed at Veracruz in 1863 to insure payment. The French, however, were not content to remain in Veracruz and eventually occupied Mexico City.

This occupation of the capital drove Juárez and his supporters into guerrilla warfare for the next four years. During this period Mexico was ruled by the Archduke Maximilian of Austria, with the support of France's Napoleon III. However,

SPANISH RULE AND MEXICAN INDEPENDENCE

> **Archduke Maximilian of Austria**
> Although the young Archduke Maximilian of Austria came to power in Mexico with the support of the conservatives in Mexico and of Napoleon III of France, he continued some of the liberal reforms begun by Benito Juárez. Maximilian restricted child labor and working hours; returned the old farming methods to Indian villages; broke the "company store" customs of the haciendas, ending their ability to keep their workers in permanent debt; and declared that peons could no longer be bought and sold like slaves for the price of that debt. But when Juárez regained power, Maximilian was made an example of, as a warning to both Europe and the U.S. not to interfere further. Juárez cast his deciding vote for Maximilian's execution on June 19, 1867. Maximilian gave each member of the firing squad a gold coin and before his death shouted, "Viva México! Viva la Independencia!"

Juárez seized power again in 1867, and he had Maximilian tried and executed.

When he died in 1872, Juárez was the first native-born Mexican leader to die naturally rather than as a result of violence. A brief break followed before General Porfirio Díaz commenced a lengthy and cruel period of dictatorship that lasted from 1876–1910. Under his rule, industries and bureaucracies began to flourish, but a majority of the common people had never lived in worse poverty or misery.

MEXICO

6 The Revolution and After

General Porfirio Díaz invited foreign investment. By the end of his period of rule, in 1910, $1.7 billion worth of foreign money had been invested in Mexico. North America invested 38 percent of this amount, 29 percent of it was from the British, and 19 percent from the French. A lot of the money went to continue the building of the famous new network of railroads that Díaz wanted seen as his major achievement. These

General Porfirio Díaz ruled Mexico for 34 years and, although during this time industry flourished and many Mexicans became wealthy, most people lived in terrible poverty.

THE REVOLUTION AND AFTER

Mines

The gold and silver for which the Spanish *conquistadores* hunted were mined mainly in the central region of Mexico. The Spaniards exhausted most of the gold mines in the colonial period, but silver still continues to be mined and wrought, the trade being centered in the colonial towns of Taxco and Guanajuato.

During the independence struggles of the early nineteenth century, production slumped and only regained former levels by 1855. However, by 1870, Guanajuato had been forced to diversify. A growing number of foreign operators increased the number of mines to 343, extracting copper, copper pyrites, tin, and mercury as well as gold and silver. Conditions in the mines were always terrible, for humans and animals alike. Mechanization and the introduction of steam power by the turn of this century reduced the colossal waste of lives as well as materials. However, poor communications, state taxes, and the need to import heavy equipment made Mexico's ore eight times as expensive at the time of the 1910 Revolution as that processed in Germany or England.

La Valenciana mine in Guanajuato was the richest of the colonial silver mines. The mine is now being reworked, and new metal and corrugated iron structures have been erected among the stone remains of earlier huts.

railroads served to transport the troops of the increasingly large army, as well as raw materials and goods from plantations to new factories. Companies from the U.S. dominated the mines in Mexico, feeding money they earned into this network. They mined not only gold and silver, which were the leading items to be mined in Mexico, but also products such as coal, lead, antimony, and copper which were easy to sell.

Díaz was very proud of the factories, but ironically they were also the site of Mexico's earliest industrial strikes, while the railroads were to be extremely helpful to the revolutionaries. Díaz made himself so loathed that it became inevitable that the people would rise up against him. They were angered by Díaz's close relationship with the U.S. Mexico's independence from Europe was very recent and had been hard to win, and now the people felt that they were being controlled by the U.S. Most of the productive land belonged to as few as 6,000 owners, and they were increasingly less likely to be Spanish than to be North American. The U.S. newspaper proprietor William Hearst acquired 2.5 million acres (1,012 million hectares) of land simply for supporting Díaz in his newspapers, and some haciendas owned by North Americans were as big as small European countries.

The fall of Díaz
However, even Hearst's protection couldn't forestall Díaz's demise. It was indirectly through the media in the U.S. that Díaz's fall began in 1910. Always a great talker, he gave a magazine in the U.S. an interview in which he declared

THE REVOLUTION AND AFTER

This photograph of the Federal Irregular Cavalry was taken in 1910. These soldiers were used to fight on the side of the government during the ensuing troubled years.

Mexico to be a true democracy that was ready for open elections. Francisco Madero, a wealthy vineyard owner from Coahuila, decided to take up the challenge and oppose the dictator for the leadership of the country. Madero promoted the idea of land reform, including giving back all stolen territories, but he relied heavily on support from the "guerrilla wing," who were the revolutionary forces that were to bring about real and lasting social and political change in Mexico.

Díaz arrested Madero to insure his own reelection. Díaz then released Madero and he fled to Texas disguised as a railroad worker. But unrest among the workers had grown due to bad conditions, and other leaders rose in support of Madero. By May 1911 Díaz was so worried about

51

MEXICO

his safety that he resigned and fled to Paris. Madero was then able to return to Mexico and win the presidency in a new election.

There were also other people interested in ruling Mexico in 1910. A Zapotec Indian named Emiliano Zapata rallied forces at this time using the slogan "Tierra y Libertad!" which means "Land and Freedom." Zapata had a strong feeling for justice born of personal outrage, but he was

Pancho Villa was a Mexican revolutionary whose band of outlaws dominated the north of the country during the Revolution of 1910. He was killed in 1923. Along with Emiliano Zapata, he is considered to be the real hero of the revolution.

THE REVOLUTION AND AFTER

illiterate and could not compete with Madero's learned writings on the subject, which included a best-selling book on *The Presidential Succession of 1910*. In the end, Zapata's sense of fairness was not enough. He mistrusted Madero's landowning interests and political quibbling, but he used his troops to support Madero. However, Madero did not last long in power. Another general who was interested in politics, named Victoriano Huerta, seized power, and Madero was shot.

Civil war
After this assassination, the revolution rapidly militarized into an all-out civil war. The revolutionaries counted on Zapata as the leader in the south of the country and his counterpart Francisco "Pancho" Villa in the north. Other revolutionary leaders included Venustiano Carranza, who like Madero was a native of Coahuila. He opposed the Díaz family's attempts to regain power, while another leader, General Alvaro Obregón, led the army against Huerta.

In 1914, Huerta was defeated and fled into exile. A provisional government, which is one that is formed until laws are worked out and a true government set up, was formed under Carranza. This provisional government gained the recognition of the U.S. Villa and Zapata mistrusted this swift alliance. It appeared that what remained of major landowning interests had come together in the provisional government. Each having commanded forces of around 50,000 troops, both Villa and Zapata now took to the mountains with small guerrilla forces.

53

MEXICO

> **The 1917 Constitution**
> The 1917 Constitution defined Mexico as a representative democracy, a federal republic. This means that the leaders of the government are elected by the people and should represent the demands of the people. In Mexico, direct elections are held for the posts of president, congressmen, state governors, and country officials. Therefore, the people can choose the person they believe to be most qualified for each position.
>
> The Congress in Mexico has two legislative bodies, which are the groups of people who discuss and form the laws of the land. The Senate is made up of 64 people, two for every state and two for the Federal District, who serve six-year terms. The Chamber of Deputies has 400 members who serve three-year terms, 300 representing citizens from electoral districts and 100 elected by proportional representation. This means that the number of people of one party represents the number of votes they get, so that the more votes gained for one group, the more people in that group can sit in the Chamber of Deputies.

It was there that, in 1919, Zapata was assassinated and, in 1923, Villa was killed as well. To the majority of Mexicans, these two indigenous leaders who had very strong characters remain the real revolutionary heroes. Ballads have been composed, songs sung, books written, and movies made about both Emiliano Zapata and Pancho Villa.

Politicians also met bloody deaths. In 1920, Carranza himself was murdered when he attempted to stop Alvaro Obregón from succeeding him as president. Obregón finally won the presidency and was acknowledged by the U.S. Since the constitution did not allow a second term, he yielded the office to his friend Plutarco Calles. But he ran again for the presidency in 1928 after he was successful in having the constitution amended to allow for another term. He then was assassinated by a devout Catholic who objected to Obregón's religious policies.

Since then no other Mexican president has been allowed to hold the position for more than one single term of office. Since then, also, there has been no party in power other than the Institutional Revolutionary Party (or PRI for short). The president is both head of government and head of state. In fact, Mexico's official name is the United Mexican States. It is made up of 31 states and a Federal District that are linked in a federation like the United States of America.

Lázaro Cárdenas
Before moving on to the present period, one other president is worthy of special note. He is Lázaro Cárdenas. Cárdenas was elected in 1934 on a platform that supported a program of reform and economic development. He encouraged the formation of labor unions for factory workers and agrarian unions for people who worked on the land. Cárdenas also emphasized social welfare programs to raise the standard of living and ended the persecution of people who had different religious views than the government. In 1938 he supported oil workers' demands for

MEXICO

After the privatization of the oil industry in April 1990, PEMEX garages like this one may become a thing of the past as the North American oil companies expand into Mexico. For over 30 years the skyscraper of the state petroleum company, the PEMEX skyscraper, has stood as a landmark in Mexico City.

higher wages and took control of 17 foreign oil companies. Although Mexico paid the companies for their assets, Mexicans were proud that their nation had taken a strong stand against foreign influence in their country. The national oil company, PEMEX, was formed, and this company was only made open to foreign investment again in 1990.

Also, when Cárdenas was president, only those born in Mexico were automatically entitled to own land there. By 1940, half of the land in Mexico that is suitable for crops was cultivated by communal villages.

7 Industry and Agriculture

Mexico ranks among the fifteen largest economies in the world. Twenty-six percent of the working population is engaged in farming and agriculture, 31 percent in the services sector, and 17 percent in industrial manufacturing.

Gold, oil, and gas
The gold mines in Mexico were stripped of all their gold. Today, only river-panning still remains as a pastime for a few adventurous and patient people, who spend hours with sievelike containers sifting sand and stones in the hope of finding gold. Oil is truly known as "the gold of the twentieth century" and is the major foreign currency-earner for Mexico. Mexico has more than enough oil to supply its own needs, so it is able to sell this valuable commodity on the world market. It is the fifth-largest producer and exporter of crude oil in the world, pumping about one billion barrels of petroleum a year. It boasts the greatest ability to refine oil out of all countries independent of the Oil-Producing & Exporting Countries, who are known as OPEC. Mexico can produce an average of 2.5 million barrels of oil daily. In addition to oil, Mexico obtains a substantial amount of energy from natural gas, ranking fifth in the world in the production of gas. Mexico's reserves of gas are estimated to be the seventh largest in the world at around 74 trillion cubic feet (2.1 trillion cubic meters).

MEXICO

Industrial control

With such wealth under Mexico's land and off its shores, it is inevitable that arguments erupt over its control. In the 1917 constitution there is a decree that is very important to the control of industry in Mexico, and even streets are named after it. This decree is Artículo 123. It seeks to define the content and character of Mexican industry. On one hand, Mexico sought to control

Sugar production is a major industry in Mexico. In this refinery at Los Mochis, Sinaloa, the sugarcane is being crushed in gigantic drums. The technology available from factory to factory varies considerably.

its own economy at the time of the revolution by forming industries that were run by the state. This meant that the state controlled the production of its natural assets, such as oil and gas, and even the running of the industries and the means by which the people could communicate, including the telephones, railroads, and more recently, the airlines. On the other hand, the rights of individual workers in these industries were strictly protected. There were a large number of laws formed by the trade unions to defend not only the working and living conditions of the worker but also his right to be respected as a "moral person."

Both moves actually made state control very strong through the next sixty years. The control of the state is only now beginning to slip. Federal laws were passed governing all major industrial and agricultural outlets, including textiles, transportation, electricity, oil, minerals, film, coffee, and sugar. These remain the most important manufactured or refined native products. Most of the industry is located in the north of the country, particularly near the Monterrey border with the U.S.

Foreign investment and trade
Since 1985, Mexico has opened up the economy to foreign investment. Carlos Salinas de Gortari, who has been president of Mexico since December 1988, is particularly eager to advance foreign investment. Trade barriers that were not linked to the taxation of goods have been lifted on 7,168 out of 8,077 products, and there has been a general promotion of Mexican exports in order to

MEXICO

> **Markets**
> At the market, while many tempting, and some not so tempting, edible goods are displayed on brightly colored shawls, even the producers can be too poor to eat the results of their own labors. On the outskirts of the market, children and old women tend grills selling *fritangas*, sauteed leftover vegetables and scraps of meat; or *tamales*, steamed cornmeal and other remnants wrapped in corn husks.
>
> "Moctezuma's revenge" is the name popularly given to the stomach upsets that Mexicans say are suffered by tourists. The upset is commonly the result of eating stale refried food or drinking contaminated water.

compete with foreign goods. The peso is not worth nearly as much as the dollar, and the U.S. can afford to buy a lot of Mexico's goods, which means that Mexico can sell its goods easily outside the country and gain money for them. Mexicans themselves sometimes find it hard to buy many goods, as so much of their produce has been exported and the prices at home go up when there are fewer goods available.

Agriculture and trade

What grows on the land is clearly as important as what lies beneath it. By 1945, 35 years after the revolution, a minimum of 49 acres (20 hectares) of land had been distributed to each of two million peasants and the major haciendas had been broken up. It was no longer true, as an advertisement in the U.S. once had it, that "United Fruit owns the biggest and richest

INDUSTRY AND AGRICULTURE

orchards in Mexico." After the revolution's acts of buying the industries and land from private and foreign owners, only the state of Veracruz has persisted in having the typical Caribbean-style plantations of palm fruits and cane fields.

A more common agricultural pattern by the mid-twentieth century is that of a mixed local economy, in which many goods are produced close to home so that the people can trade with each other. Small farms produce staple crops such as rice, beans, and corn. Some people, mainly in the north of Mexico, raise animals on a ranch and others grow additional fruit and vegetables to take to market. Sugar, coffee, and cotton, in contrast to the goods at the market, need to be planted on a larger scale, and they are usually grown close to where they are processed in a mixed agricultural and industrial complex.

The Oaxaca Valley supports a variety of crops, including the castor oil plant. This grows well in dry regions and is an excellent source of oil for lubricants.

Mexico's principal crops are corn, sorghum, coffee, sugarcane, wheat, beans (particularly soybeans and red kidney beans, although pintos, chickpeas, and black-eyed peas are widely grown), rice, barley, cotton, and safflower, the oil of which is used in margarines. There is a small but growing luxury export industry of food items ranging from shark livers and lobsters to strawberries and cantaloupes.

Tourism

Luxury food items are closely tied to tourism, Mexico's fastest-growing industry. The last count, dated 1984, listed 2,269 highly ranked hotels with 155,618 rooms. Five years later there were estimated to be twice as many hotels, often located in new resorts. Each president sets up his own resort and the last president, Miguel de la Madrid, promoted Cancún as the Caribbean counterpart to the Pacific coast's Acapulco.

By far the majority of foreigners (90 percent) visiting Mexico come from the U.S. and Canada. British tourism has increased dramatically in a recent five-year period, rising from 10,500 in 1985 to over 70,000 in 1989. The preferred destinations have traditionally been Mexico City and Acapulco, although other resorts are growing in popularity. These include archaeological sites such as Cozumel and Uxmal on the Yucatán peninsula, Oaxaca in the south, Guanajuato in the high plains, Puerto Vallarta and Ixtapa on the Pacific coast, and the colonial towns of Taxco, Cholula, San Miguel de Allende, and San Cristóbal de las Casas. The tourists and the hotels they stay in stand in contrast to the many

INDUSTRY AND AGRICULTURE

Tourism is rapidly becoming a major industry in Mexico. There are numerous new resorts as well as well-established ones, such as Acapulco. Some high-rise hotels that fringe the edge of Hornos beach reflect Aztec architecture.

thousands of poor refugees who flood across Mexico's borders from politically troubled Central American countries, often to find only the crudest shelter near the Guatemalan frontiers.

According to the latest available statistics (1987) 5,407,000 tourists visited Mexico that year; their average length of stay was ten days; and the total amount of money made by the tourist industry was $2.27 billion. By contrast, less than half that number of Mexican tourists left home; those who did, stayed away only a week; and spent a total of only $784 million. Therefore, through tourism the Mexican economy had gained $1.49 billion that stayed in the country as it was not spent by Mexican tourists going to other countries.

8 Travel in a Land of Mountains and Lakes

Mexico's very complex geography makes communications particularly difficult. There is no river linking the two coasts and, unlike Panama to the south, no canal has been dug, or is planned to be dug, to cut through the country. The mountain ranges to the east and west are so steep that only relatively restricted rail connections have been built between such major towns as Mexico City, Guadalajara, San Luís Potosí, León, or Cuernavaca. Distances between the towns are so vast that roads, despite modern networks, can be slow to travel. It is worth bearing in mind that while it is only 35 miles (56 kilometers) from the capital to Cuernavaca as the crow flies, the journey involves a climb of nearly 10,000 feet (3,048 meters) on leaving Mexico City and dropping a dramatic 5,500 feet (1,676 meters) into the capital of the state of Morelos.

The easiest way to reach the U.S. is to travel along the central plateau between the two main mountain ranges. In the west, there are rail and road links across the Sierra Madre Occidental from Guadalajara to the port of Mazatlán on the Pacific, then northward through the Nogales desert. The Sierra Madre Oriental, to the east, contains a pass running inland from Tampico. It allows for road and railroad access north to the industrial center of Monterrey, and from the southern port and trading center of Veracruz inland to the Valley of Mexico.

TRAVEL IN A LAND OF MOUNTAINS AND LAKES

Buses are a very popular form of transportation in Mexico and they go everywhere—even to the most remote villages. All the luggage, plus vegetables and fruit for the market, travel on the roof. Chickens, goats, and other livestock are piled inside with the people.

Highways

Mainly because of the importance of trade, and increasingly because of tourism, routes southward from the U.S. have become necessary. Many new highways have been constructed in Mexico in the last 20 years. Now over 62,140 miles (100,000 kilometers) of paved roads, and considerably more miles of unpaved roads, transport 80 percent of goods and over 97 percent of passengers traveling through Mexico. Although several international car rental firms operate out of major cities, there are few Mexican ones, and a minority of Mexicans own their own cars. Buses go everywhere. On the major routes the buses are often air-conditioned and modern, and always a cheap means of travel. Buses on the

MEXICO

The Metro
The underground rail system in Mexico City is known as the Metro. It is both the biggest and the newest mass transit system of any capital city in the world. The Metro's other claims to fame are that it is also the highest, as the city itself is so far above sea level, and it has the cheapest fares in the world at 50 pesos (two cents) a ride. The Metro is surprisingly safe as it is heavily patrolled by a special transportation police force, and some cars are reserved for women and children only.

minor routes are often old and rickety! The Volkswagen car factory in Mexico City, however, is huge, and the capital seems to be full of "Beetles," which have become the standard taxi as well as the most popular private car.

Travel by air
Mexico boasts more airports than any other country in the whole of Latin America. It has 30 international and 20 domestic airports. The main international airlines fly both into the capital and

TRAVEL IN A LAND OF MOUNTAINS AND LAKES

Air travel is widely used in Mexico because journeys through the mountains take so long. There are a number of small domestic airlines such as Air Cozumel.

to such resorts as Acapulco on the Pacific coast and Cancún on the Caribbean. Mexico's main domestic airline is called Mexicana, and the international one is called AeroMexico. In Mexico, airline prices are cheap, and traveling by air can save a lot of time. A flight that takes only 40 minutes, such as the one from Mexico City to Tuxtla in the state of Chiapas, can replace a bus journey of over 18 hours.

From the air, the snow-coated summit of Popocatépetl can be seen. Popocatépetl is a volcano only 43 miles (75 kilometers) southeast of Mexico City, alongside a ring of dormant "flame throwers." It is also possible to visualize the central basin of Mexico as the lake it was when the Spaniards arrived in the sixteenth century.

67

9 Health, Education, and Welfare

According to some people who have studied Mexican homes, in a typical rural Mexican family the father is expected to make the decisions and to give orders. Meanwhile, the mother works at keeping home life running smoothly according to her husband's wishes. Ever since the revolution, the government of Mexico appears to have taken on a similar role to that of the father. The Mexican government seems to try to treat the entire population as its family in its provision of health, education, and welfare services. In order to provide good services, there are constant problems to be solved in ensuring there is enough money available to pay for the services and that plans are administered properly. Also, the government often has to counter the traditional beliefs of the people.

The government uses a number of different sources for funds to pay for the services it runs. Some of the money has been gained from foreign trade and national industries, which are run by the state, but most of it comes from the people themselves. Workers have to pay into an insurance fund when they are paid so that they have the right to use the services that the government provides. The employers have to pay a contribution for each worker as well.

The government does not try to make any profit from national services and works with tight budgets keeping costs down and offering basic services. This means that it has to compete with new business-run private services that cost people a lot of money to use but can afford to offer better service. Also, the government's plans for national services are on such a big scale that not every region may benefit from them due to difficulties in reaching remote areas. Even in the 1970s, nearly two generations after the revolution's first campaigns for social justice, there were still few doctors and teachers in many of the rural areas.

The lack of teachers in rural areas is also the result of old prejudices against an education system that rarely met the needs of a rural lifestyle. Often children attend school for just a year or two, until they can read and write and can do basic math. The children are then withdrawn from school to help with the essential work in the fields or in the home.

As for health, many Mexican families still consider traditional healers, called *curanderos*, to be adequate in meeting their health care needs. These healers often use herbal treatments and add a religious touch to their medical knowledge. They also frequently cost less than the amount of money people have to pay into national insurance for the use of the health service. It is a common sight to see mothers with sick infants begging outside pharmacies for money to buy medicine. In some cases, it is often better for them to go to the curandero to buy lemon balm, to make their babies tea to cure such things as diarrhea, than to give a sickly child strong drugs. The dehydration that results from diarrhea is the most common killer of infants under one year old. So, in Mexico

MEXICO

two systems exist alongside one another: the system offered by the Health, Education, and Social Security departments of the government since the revolution, and the traditional family structures to which a substantial number of the people still adhere.

National education

In terms of national education, Mexico has proved largely successful in teaching basic skills.

Since the revolution, many more children have been educated. In Mexico secondary schools are quite crowded and teaching is very traditional with few visual aids.

70

HEALTH, EDUCATION, AND WELFARE

Eighty-eight percent of all Mexicans are now literate in Spanish, which is a huge contrast with the number of people who were literate in the 1940s and 1950s. Schooling takes place according to the number of years completed rather than according to age. Pupils spend six years in *primaria*, three in *secundaria,* and another four in *preparatoria.* Pupils starting at age six, who may already have been taught basic skills in nursery school, rarely complete their schooling before the age of nineteen or twenty. If they then continue their education at a university, most degrees take another five years to obtain.

Schools are normally open from 8 a.m., and occasionally from 7 a.m. straight through until a late lunchtime at around 2 p.m. There is a break at about 11 a.m. for a snack, and the afternoons are kept free for additional classes and sports. Uniforms are hardly ever compulsory, although many younger children wear similar clothing. All state schools admit both boys and girls.

The state provides 70 percent of schools. The private schools are owned by religious orders and financed by fee-paying parents. In the nineteenth century liberals sought to limit the Church's control over education, but no reforms of this sort were successfully enacted. The leaders of the revolution continued to press for public education. In 1934 the socialist President Lázaro Cárdenas brought out laws stating that no monks, priests, or nuns may teach in the schools they run and Christian religious education is forbidden. A considerable slice of the national budget goes to support education, and the Mexican government spends more of its money

MEXICO

When University City in Mexico City was established, the celebrated Mexican artist Juan O'Gorman was commissioned to design a mural. His mural depicts the history of Mexican culture.

on education than in any other Latin American country except Costa Rica.

Health care

Health care also reflects the ideals left by the revolution. The health service introduced at the time of the revolution was primarily formed to benefit workers in a country where industry was growing very quickly. The health program in Mexico has two parts. One system is for people who work for state-run businesses or industries, and the other for those who work for private organizations. There is a nationwide system of national insurance and public hospitals. Unfortunately, due to isolation people in rural areas have never been able to make much use of

HEALTH, EDUCATION, AND WELFARE

Street Children
Many children leave school after the primary grades and work at night amid dangerous traffic on the streets in the capital. They can be divided into three groups: children of the urban poor who work to support their families; those who have drifted in from rural areas and sleep on the streets in the care of old women, often referred to as "grandmothers," and those children who eke out an existence with no adult support of any kind. Despite the efforts of the increasing number of charities, these children are outside the state education and welfare services, and their numbers are continually growing. It is now estimated that as many as one and a half million Mexicans are "street children."

this health system. Other groups in the population not helped by this system include the elderly, who may not have paid national insurance contributions if they have worked for themselves on the land, the unemployed, who cannot get jobs and do not earn money or pay national insurance, and people in need such as the poor and homeless of whom Mexico has increasing numbers.

Nonetheless, health in Mexico has shown dramatic overall improvement since the revolution. Whereas in 1910, 300 out of every 1,000 babies born in Mexico died at or near birth, by 1989 the number of infant deaths had dropped

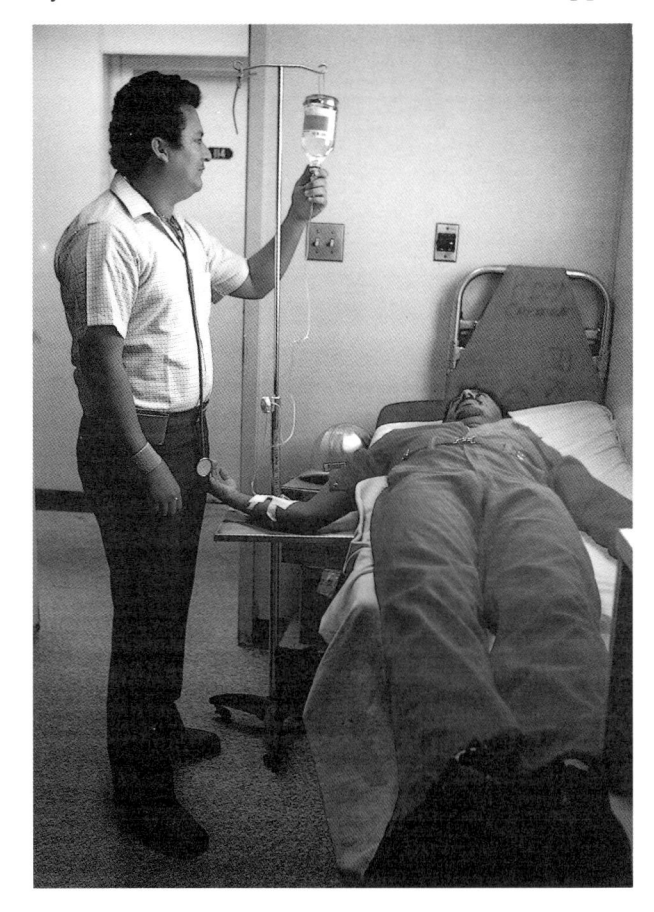

Health care in Mexico is variable. It has greatly improved since the revolution, but whereas medical care for workers, such as this oil rig worker, is excellent and is paid for by the state or the company, many people, especially in rural areas, have very little medical help at all.

HEALTH, EDUCATION, AND WELFARE

to 42 per 1,000. The general mortality rate, which was 33 per 1,000 in 1920 also dropped, to 10.3 in 1964. By 1989 it was down to 6. To some extent this has been due to the establishment of health clinics or hospitals in each of Mexico's 31 states, although there are more in some areas than others. Also, the state took over the running of the drug industry, which helped reduce prices dramatically. It meant that common medicines such as aspirin and penicillin could be bought over the counter from the local pharmacist. Often the pharmacist has a position of responsibility in which he or she makes a general diagnosis about what illness a person has and is able to supply the drugs needed to cure the patient.

Social security

Social security is also mainly targeted at industrial workers, and the powerful National Federation of Farmers has won considerable allowances in terms of payments for workplace accidents and pension programs as well. However, there is still no national unemployment benefit or pension for those who, like most of the women, do not have paid work outside the home or the small patch of farmland on which they grow some crops. People who work for responsible employers who pay insurance are entitled to free transportation to the hospital if they suffer a workplace-related illness or accident. Besides the insurance policy, the employer also pays for all medical care while the worker is in the hospital, for medicines, and also for care needed once the worker has left the hospital. The worker is also guaranteed weekly wages for up to 72 weeks if the accident is so serious that he or she cannot work. If the worker is permanently injured and unable to work again, a lifetime pension is provided according to how much he or she was earning when the serious accident happened.

Although the Social Security system in the 1950s and 1960s extended so far as to build *colonias*, which are large municipal housing developments intended to wipe out slums on the city outskirts, many townspeople do not qualify for a home in these complexes. These people often resort to the "black market" to make money to live on. Working in the black market means selling what they can gather, or what they can afford to buy on the streets. Some of these people send their children out to beg for money that the rest of the family can use.

10 Home and Away

Mexican homes vary greatly from city to countryside, rich to poor, and region to region. Generally the old colonial towns preserve perhaps the most popular middle-class houses of the last five centuries, built around a central courtyard. The older houses still have wells in the center and balconies jutting out from the upper floors, supported underneath by arches. The arches give these homes the air of a cloister and make the patio a cool retreat from the noise of the streets and the darkness of the downstairs kitchens. Sometimes larger colonial houses are partitioned so that several families live around the same courtyard. Washing and cooking

> **Mexican Cuisine**
> Mexico is renowned for having one of the most elaborate cuisines in the Americas: Moctezuma was said to have had 1,000 dishes a day to choose from! Some Indian foods have given their names to other languages: tomato, potato, avocado, papaya, banana, chocolate, and cocoa among them. The national dish of Puebla, *molé*, involves coating a turkey in a rich, unsweetened chocolate sauce. Chicken, pork, and spicy sausage are the meats that ordinary people are most likely to eat, usually wrapped with lettuce and cheese in a *tortilla* (corn pancake) that serves as both plate and napkin. Chili is almost as constant an accompaniment as tortilla to most savory dishes. For dessert, Mexican cooking offers fruits, sherbets, and heavy, filling cakes.

MEXICO

facilities may be shared, along with the upkeep of the plants that Mexicans often keep hanging from balconies, crowding the banisters, and filling the central flower beds.

The homeless and the slums

Larger cities and border towns often become the site of slums and shantytowns. Many of the shelters in shantytowns are so temporary that they can literally be put up and taken down overnight as families get forced to relocate with their rough supplies of planks, corrugated iron, and plastic sheeting. Some city-dwellers, particularly people newly arrived in the city and the frontier refugees who have come across the border from another country without any money, are so poor that they have no shelter at all. These

There are millions of children in Mexico City who are living in very poor accommodations, either in derelict slums like these children, or shantytowns where their temporary homes are made mostly of scrap materials.

HOME AND AWAY

> **Traditional Homes**
> Traditional homes vary enormously. They are all created with the resources of their local environment. Huts are either built from packed clay or woven with branches or palms, and thatched roofs are supported on forked wooden stakes. In regions where they don't even have these materials, such as in the desert north of Mexico, people live under whatever shelter they find. Some people live in the caves of northern Chichuahua. Others are nomads who travel from place to place, living in tents or even sometimes just covering themselves with serapes and sleeping among their animals.

people have to cover themselves with their *serapes*, which are poncholike blankets that can be draped or worn to keep warm. They huddle together against the bitter cold at night and sleep on the streets. A relatively new feature in the capital is the number of "roof-dwellers." These are people who literally live on the roofs of houses without the residents below knowing that they are there. Sometimes roof-dwellers move on every night, and sometimes they live in semipermanent shacks. When the roof-dwellers are groups of young boys, they make a point of picking dangerously high skyscrapers to sleep on. This adds the spice of excitement and selected risk to the situation.

Vacations and fiestas
The idea of vacations is a very modern one in Mexico and most of the people in the countryside

MEXICO

don't take them. Mexico attempts to make up for the lack of vacations abroad by having 365 one-day fiestas on its calendar. Fiestas are celebrated like carnivals, which were introduced to Mexico by the Spanish. People can choose which ones to celebrate, although some are celebrated by everyone in the country.

While some Mexicans certainly do travel

Mexicans enjoy fiestas so much they have them on every possible occasion! It is an opportunity for joyous singing and dancing and for wearing the beautiful traditional costumes. These girls are from Tehunteaca in Oaxaca, a region famous for its embroidery.

HOME AND AWAY

abroad, mainly within the Americas, school breaks are often a time for sending the children back to relatives still living in the countryside. There, especially during the months the children are out of school in the summer and for religious festivals, there are bound to be fiestas for them to attend. Often these are to celebrate a local saint—a patron who may look suspiciously like an earlier Indian wise man or warrior.

Alternatively, the fiesta may be connected to the child's own name day if he or she was named after the community's own patron saint. Sometimes fiestas are linked to the festivities attached to a girl becoming a *quinceañera*, or coming of age. There are also *piñata* parties, which are held for younger children on birthdays or name days. At these parties the child is blindfolded and given a stick with which he or she tries to hit the piñata, a large clay pot colorfully

Coming of Age
When a Mexican girl turns fifteen, she becomes a *quinceañera*, which brings several privileges. One of the advantages is that she no longer has to share a bedroom with any younger brothers and sisters! Mexico must be one of the few countries that has this "rite of passage" celebration for girls and not boys, unlike in Jewish communities, which celebrate both. When a girl is fifteen, she can also expect a later bedtime and permission to take part in another custom called the *paseo*. This means going out on a Sunday evening and circling the town square, arms linked with her girlfriends, until she meets a boy she wants to spend some time with.

decorated as an animal or other figure and slung from a high rope. If the child does not split the piñata, the turn passes to another child. Once the pot breaks open, candies and little gifts shower down on the children, who scramble for them.

Sports and leisure

As with the fiestas, many sporting pastimes derived from the Spanish. Bullfights are among the most popular pastimes. Almost every town has a bullfight as a Sunday afternoon's entertainment. That means there are at least 250 in Mexico on a Sunday. Mexico City's stadium, with its seating capacity of 50,000, is the largest in the world.

Horses, which were first brought to Mexico by the Spaniards, are used in many of the same type of competitions and races as they are in the U.S. One of the most popular uses of horses is for rodeos. In a rodeo, cowboys ride wild horses to see how long they can stay on. In Mexico rodeos are sometimes called *charreadas*. Country-and-western music, called *canciones rancheras*, is played at these events and it is every bit as much fun to dance to and as sentimental as that played north of the border in the U.S.

Ever since the early years of this century, the favorite ball game has been soccer. This appears to give Mexico an unfair advantage when its teams play neighboring Central American countries where baseball is more popular. Other countries have given Mexican players bribes and bought players from Mexican teams. It is a sport for the younger generation and it seems fitting that the Universitarios, a team made up of

HOME AND AWAY

university students, is one of the most successful soccer teams in Mexico.

Other popular team ball games include basketball, volleyball, hockey, polo, and pelota. Pelota is also called jai-alai or *frontón* and was originally a Catalan game. It is similar to the game of squash. For some reason it is especially popular in the border town of Tijuana, although Mexico City's pelota court, which is called the Frontón, seats 4,000 visitors. Boxing is a sport that often appeals to boys from the slum areas, or *barrios*, and Mexico has produced several world champion bantamweights.

Music and dance

Dancing and music are features of every fiesta, and here again Mexico shows an extraordinary cultural mixture. The music ranges from the

There are many traditional dances in Mexico, and one of the most spectacular is performed at Papantla. A group of Totonac Indians, known as Voladores *or* Flying Dancers, *perform by weaving around each other while suspended from the top of a pole 89 feet (27 meters) high.*

sound of traditional Indian string or wind instruments, which play sad tunes, to classical Spanish guitars, or to noisy *mariachi* bands, which come from the Mexican countryside. Indian dances are rooted in religion, and they are often as elaborate as the religious beliefs. A group of Totonac Indians perform "Flying Dances," with four men weaving their way in and out of one another, hanging upside-down from a pole 89 feet (27 meters) above the ground. Other dances involve complex formations, the women wearing brilliantly colored skirts and the men in elaborate feathered headdresses. The emphasis is always on people dancing together rather than on individual performances.

The Independence movement and art
It was only with the Independence movement in the last century that Mexico received praise from all over the world for its success in art. Mexico became particularly famous in the last century because of the great murals that were being painted, for being the best at photography in Latin America, for having great poets and people who wrote excellent essays, and for its modernist architecture. Yet there is still a tradition in the world that calls what Europeans create "the arts," and what the Indians create "crafts." It is only very recently that crafts such as weaving and embroidery, ceramics and pottery, bone-carving and silver-work, which are popular art forms of the Mexican culture, have begun to be properly appreciated. Galleries and a Museum of Popular Culture now show all forms.

11 Religion and Culture

Mexico sees itself as bringing together ancient indigenous civilizations and European traditions, with beliefs and religious practices in the country that come from both. Just as *mestizaje* is the word used to summarize this blending among the people, so in terms of religion the merging has come to be known as syncretism, and in culture as a synthesis.

In practice, of course, nothing as neat as the sort of blending that happens when a can of paint is mixed up or ingredients in a cake are mixed actually takes place. Indians in some parts of the country preserve their ways and beliefs without much change. In other areas, and particularly in

The interior of the Basilica de la Soledad, Oaxaca, is a fine example of the interior of a Mexican church. The style adopted from the Europeans is baroque, with plenty of gold and silver leaf and numerous statues.

some of the colonial towns or the richer city suburbs, the life-styles are the same as almost anywhere in the southern Americas, because the races have mixed their ways. The most curious mixtures, however, are those where modern practices hardly change ancient beliefs and symbolisms. One of the most common similarities between the ancient and the modern world in Mexico is found in the worship of Catholic saints. The saints look and act very like great Indian leaders.

Separating religion from culture
The idea of separating religion from culture is a recent one. Among the ancient Indians in Mexico, just as among the native North Americans or the Roman and Greek civilizations in Europe, the arts, sciences, architecture, education, and even drinking and dancing were all aspects of religion. Even so-called "primitive" desert nomads had their own customs or traditional practices. The Seri have preserved their worship of the moon and sun, and also of the pelican and turtle, which they both honor and hunt. When a German missionary saw the Seri in 1685, he said, "Here are a people altogether without faith or religion and who live like cattle." He was wrong, for these people had very strong beliefs.

The Aztec practice of daily human sacrifice, which was to keep their sun-god happy, shocked the Spaniards. Like most colonizers, the Spaniards had little respect for beliefs they did not bother to understand. Nonetheless, the emperor Moctezuma was more interested in religion than warfare, and he welcomed the

RELIGION AND CULTURE

> **Banner of the Virgin of Guadalupe**
> Following the visions of Juan Diego, a poor sixteenth-century Indian, an immense basilica, a church looking like a royal palace, was built on the outskirts of Mexico City to honor the Virgin Mary. Diego saw her "surrounded by tongues of light" and she is always shown in this way. Each year six million pilgrims visit Juan Diego's shrine where the cloak, on which the Virgin imprinted her image, is preserved. Many come on her feast day of December 12, making the journey from the city center after long fasting and on their knees in an act of penance. This was the first shrine to be built, if not to an indigenous saint, at least to an indigenous apparition! This explains much of its great popularity. A bigger and newer basilica has just been built.

Spaniards as messengers of Quetzalcóatl, god of culture and beauty, rather than of the principal god Huitzilopochtli, god of the sun and war.

When the Spanish tried to convert the Indians to the Catholic faith, syncretism set in. Many communities paid lip service to Catholicism but sought secretly to preserve their traditional beliefs. Plenty of modern examples of this persist: in religious processions loaves baked in the form of former gods are carried as altar-bread; Indian music and dances to the old ceremonies are preserved; the churches are used for libations, which is the pouring of alcohol in honor of God, and for chanting. Roman Catholicism is still very much the dominant national religion, with over 80 percent of the population baptized in it. As in the rest of Latin America, Protestant and

MEXICO

evangelical sects from the U.S. are increasingly trying to convert people to their religions. There is also a small group of Jews in Mexico, and many of them are of Russian or Middle Eastern origin rather than Spanish. The state has tried to reduce the power of the Church, but religion remains very much a part of the national culture. Many people in Mexico go to church every Sunday.

Death and dreams
The Day of the Dead, November 2, is one of the biggest annual festivals in the Catholic calendar. Processions of relatives of the dead dress in white

Murals by Diego Rivera
Rivera was a member of the Communist party (from which he was eventually expelled) and combined political activity with his art. Although most famous for his murals in Mexico and the U.S. (including those at Rockefeller Center in New York and Mexico's National Palace), Rivera also painted many pictures and made mosaics.

The murals by Diego Rivera at the National Palace in Mexico City are a great tourist attraction. They show the development of Mexican culture both before and after the revolution.

RELIGION AND CULTURE

On November 2, Mexicans celebrate the Day of the Dead. It is one of their most important festivals. In Mixquic, models of skeletons are floated on rafts of flowers on the waters of the lakes as part of the remembrance ceremonies.

and make their way to the cemetery at night, placing flowers and lit candles on the graves. Children get a day off from school to buy and sell sugar skulls and skeletons iced with traditional patterns and the names of the dead. Dreams are taken seriously by rural *curanderos* (healers) and *brujos* (people who cast spells) and are believed to reveal "another reality" rather than simply the workings of a person's unconscious.

12 Mexico Today — and Tomorrow

Mexico's greatest problem is its foreign debt. After the heady days of the oil boom of the 1960s when it had the fastest-growing economy in Latin America, Mexico's economic growth rate dropped to zero. This is hard for the government to deal with, especially at a time when the rapidly expanding birth rate, which is about the same as India's, generates the need for nearly a million new jobs a year.

In July 1989, Mexico's foreign debt was $103 billion, including $53 billion owed to commercial lending institutions. To avoid meeting such crippling interest charges and business debts, a complex repayment deal was put in place in order to stop the flow of Mexican pesos into dollar accounts abroad. This is the first time banks that lend people money have agreed to such a massive reduction in public debts. The reduction was 35 percent of the money borrowed.

Foreign investment
The slide of the peso against other currencies, while bad news for Mexican consumers, favors foreign investment. The U.S. remains by far the largest investor, followed by Britain, then Germany, France, and Japan. The "top ten" investors must be approximately the same as a century ago, and it is striking that none of Mexico's Latin American or Caribbean neighbors are among them.

The drug problem and human rights

Another of Mexico's problems is drug production and trafficking. In the north of the country and the Gulf of Mexico, helicopters are part of frequent joint operations between the U.S. and Mexican antidrug squads searching out fields of marijuana. While Mexico's armed forces comprise 100,000 troops, about 25 percent are given the chore of controlling the production and smuggling of drugs. Mexican people are proud that the rest of the troops are mainly employed on "socially oriented" programs, such as helping earthquake or flood victims, and that Mexico has never started a war.

As an extension of using its troops for peaceful means, Mexico is a member of the United Nations and has promoted its doctrine of people throughout the world helping each other. Moreover, it has used its concern for human rights to promote conventional and nuclear disarmament at both a regional and global level. Ever since the 1967 "Tlatelolco Treaty," a nuclear-free zone in a heavily populated region was created in Mexico. Being nuclear-free is something Mexico has attempted to promote throughout Latin America.

Pollution and environmental damage

Finally, pollution and environmental damage are growing dangerously in Mexico. Already the atmospheric pollution in the capital, created in part by five million cars, is so acute that schools have to close during January when the temperature is lowest and the cold air is trapped near the ground. This pollution has created

MEXICO

In the earthquake of 1985, 20,000 people lost their lives. Most of these people were in Mexico City where hospitals, parking garages, and office buildings like these collapsed like packs of cards. After the earthquake the emergency services took a long time to restore order and were angrily accused of inefficiency.

epidemics of throat and chest infections among the weakest members of society, including children. Also, it means the loss of a long summer break for schoolchildren, in return for a month off after Christmas.

Previous policies that favored sending landless peasants from the infertile north to seek out self-sufficiency in the south created a "slash-and-burn" mentality as the people burned down areas of wild vegetation in order to create small plots of land to build on and to farm. As a result, in Oaxaca, Guerrero, and Chiapas between 40 and 60 percent of the forests have been destroyed.

Political and economic stability

Still, starvation and disease are scarcer in Mexico than in most other Latin American countries. The

MEXICO TODAY—AND TOMORROW

Perhaps these students will be involved in later years in helping their country resolve some of its many and increasing problems.

political and economic situations are more stable, even in the face of real problems. However, corruption and bribery are common allegations regarding police and politicians, and recent elections have been tainted with charges of fraud and forgery.

The future

Mestizaje is a real achievement, permitting many Mexicans to be proud of their dual heritage and to respect the legacy of the revolution. This is the case despite the inescapable fact that the richer classes are clearly whiter than the brown-skinned rural poor or the urban beggars. Some of the recognition, and even praise, of the Indian legacy has come through the arts. In the 1920s and 1930s, the muralists and painters like David Siqueiros, Diego Rivera, and Rufino Tamayo became internationally known.

It is often said that a country's future lies in its children. In Mexico's case the 500-year-long process of mestizaje has meant that, unlike some neighboring countries (including the U.S.), racial tension is not a significant issue.

Culturally, this mixture has endowed Mexico with a wealth of arts, artifacts, and architecture. Politically, Mexico needs to move beyond the stranglehold of the aptly named Institutional Revolutionary party, toward a much more representative system.

Economically, the range of its major industries has allowed Mexico to escape some of the worst ravages common to Latin American countries that are stricken by international debts. Only recently, however, has Mexico begun to use the major resource of its past to promote its swelling tourist and property industries. Perhaps Mexico's past will provide answers to some of the questions regarding its future.

Index

Acapulco 15-16
agriculture 11, 21-23, 38-39, 60–62
archaeology 62
area 9
arts and crafts 42, 84, 88, 93
Aztecs 5, 30-36, 86-87

Baja California 8, 15
bananas 16, 22, 39
Belize 9
birds 17-19
boundaries 5, 8-9
bullfighting 82

Cárdenas, Lázaro 55-56, 71
Chiapas region 10-11, 15
chili 22, 77
civil war 43, 53-54
climate 11, 12, 13-16
coastline 10, 11
coffee 39, 59, 61
communications 10, 49, 59, 64
Constitution of 1917 54-55, 58
Cortés, Hernán 10, 25, 32, 33-36, 40
cotton 38-39, 61
currency 59-60, 90

debt 90, 94
deserts 10-11, 15
Díaz, Porfirio 47-48, 50-51
disease 25-26, 41

distance 64
drugs 75, 91

earthquakes 11-13
economy 55-56, 57-63, 90
education 69-72
energy sources 57, 59
exports, 21, 59-60, 62

fiestas 79-82, 83
fishing 21
food 21-23, 60-62, 77
forests 10-11, 92

Gortari, Carlos Salinas de 59
government 53-55, 58-59, 68-69
 social policy 68-69
Guadalajara 12
Guadalupe, Treaty of 44-45
Guatemala 9, 31, 63
Gulf of Mexico 8

health and welfare 68-70, 72-76
Hidalgo y Costilla, Miguel 43, 44
homeless people 73-74, 78-79
housing 76-79

Independence movement 43-46, 84
Indians 9, 24-28, 35, 36-37, 84, 86, 87
Institutional Revolutionary Party (PRI) 55, 94

Juárez, Benito 45-47

95

land ownership 37-39, 56, 60-61
language 5, 7, 9, 28

Madero, Francisco 51-53
markets 60
Maximilian, Archduke of Austria 46-47
Maya 8-9, 26, 30-32
mestizo (mestizaje) 28-29, 43, 85, 93-94
Mexico City 10, 12-13, 14, 44, 46, 62, 64
mining 42, 49, 50, 57
mortality rate 74-75
mountains 10, 11, 64
music and dance 83-87

nuclear disarmament 91

Oaxaca 10, 23, 62
Obregón, Alvaro 53, 54-55
oil and gas 55-57, 59, 90

plants and crops 21-23, 39, 61, 62
pollution 21, 91-92
Popocatépetl 12, 67
population 9-10, 26, 32
ports 11
pyramids 24

refugees 63
religion 32-33, 40-42, 85-88
  Catholicism 40-42, 86-87
  Indian 32, 85
Revolution of 1910 29
Rivera, Diego 88, 94
rivers 8, 21

San Andreas faultline 12-13
seasons 15
slavery 27, 28-29, 37, 39
soccer 82-83
Spanish conquest 7, 10, 27-28, 32-37
Spanish rule 37, 40-43
sports and leisure 82-83
street children 73
sugarcane 39, 59, 61

Tenochtitlán 5, 33-36
Three Years War 46
tourism 11, 62-63, 94
trade and industry 57-61, 68
trade unions 59
transportation 10, 48, 59, 64-67
  air 59, 66-67
  rail 10, 48-50, 59, 66
  road 10, 64-66

United States 5, 7, 44, 50, 64-65, 90

volcanoes 11-12, 67
Veracruz 16, 32, 46, 61, 64
Villa, Pancho 53-54

wildlife 17-21

Zapata, Emiliano 52-54
Zapoteca Indians 26-27

© Heinemann Children's Reference 1991
This edition originally published 1991 by Heinemann Children's Reference, a division of Heinemann Educational Books, Ltd.